It was Christmas Eve.
The children were excited, but
   Mum was hot and Dad was cross.
'Christmas is hard work,' said Dad.

Dad put up some decorations.
He wanted the children to help, but
   they didn't want to.
They were watching television.

Dad turned off the television.
'Oh!' said Kipper. 'We were
    watching a good programme.'
'It's time to help,' said Dad.

Just then, Wilf and Wilma came.
They had brought presents for Biff,
  Chip and Kipper.
'We can help later,' said Chip.

Biff and Chip had presents for
  Wilf and Wilma.
'Don't open them until
  tomorrow,' said Biff.

The magic key began to glow.
'It's time for a magic adventure,'
   said Chip.
'I hope it's a Christmas adventure.'

The magic key took the children to
the land of Father Christmas.
'Hooray!' said Wilf. 'We can tell
Father Christmas what to bring us.'

The children were excited.
They all wanted special presents.
'I want a new bike,' said Kipper.
'I want a new skateboard,' said Biff.

The children rang the door bell.
They rang and rang, but
    nobody came to the door.
'That's funny!' said Chip.

The children looked for Father
   Christmas, but he was not there.
There was nobody there.
'Where is everyone?' asked Wilma.

The children were disappointed.
'It's not fair,' said Chip.
'I wanted to ask Father Christmas for
   a computer.'

The children looked for Father
    Christmas.
They came to his house.
'Maybe he's in here,' said Kipper.

The children went inside.
An old man was asleep in a chair.
'It's Father Christmas,' said Wilf.
'Why is he asleep in a chair?'

Biff looked at the date.
'It's the 25th of December,' she said.
'Father Christmas must be tired.
He's been at work all night.'

14

Suddenly, Father Christmas woke up.
'What are you doing here?' he asked.
'It's Christmas Day.
Did I forget to call at your house?'

Father Christmas hadn't put up
   his decorations.
'I've been too busy.
It's the same every year,' he said.

Father Christmas had
    no Christmas dinner.
'I didn't have time,' he said.
'Children want so many presents.'

The children were sorry for
   Father Christmas.
They found a Christmas tree and
   put it up.

They found some decorations and
  put them up.
'I haven't had decorations up for
  years,' said Father Christmas.

Wilma and Chip made some strawberry
  jam sandwiches.
Father Christmas found some
  lemonade and some crackers.

Father Christmas put on his
   red coat.
'Ho! Ho! Ho!' he laughed.
Everyone cheered.

'Thank you,' said Father Christmas.
'Most children just want things, but
you've given me a good Christmas.'

Just then, the key began to glow.
'Happy Christmas,' said everyone.
'Goodbye,' said Father Christmas.
'Thank you for everything.'

The magic took the children home.
It was Christmas Eve again.
'What else can we do to help?'
    asked Chip.